For Joey
—L.B.

To my husband, Matthew, for his love and support
—W.K.

Text copyright © 2016 by Lauren Bradshaw
Illustrations copyright © 2016 by Wednesday Kirwan
Book design by Sara Gillingham Studio

Library of Congress Control Number available
ISBN: 978-1-937359-94-2

Printed in China

10 9 8 7 6 5 4 3 2 1

Cameron Kids is an imprint of
Cameron + Company
6 Petaluma Blvd., Suite B6
Petaluma, CA 94952
www.cameronbooks.com

WALNUT ANIMAL SOCIETY

HENRY'S BRIGHT IDEA

by Lauren Bradshaw

Illustrated by Wednesday Kirwan

cameron kids

Deep in the shade of a walnut grove stands
a tall tree house.

A delightful group of friends gathers here.
They call themselves the Walnut Animal Society.

Their mission is to create and to always remain curious.

Henry the Fox is a knowledgeable fellow,
known for his unique inventions.

Margaux the Kitty's many books are filled
with stories and poems she's written.

Ruthie the Deer loves to dance
like the butterflies that flutter outside.

The collection of ropes and fishing poles
belongs to adventurous *Chester the Raccoon.*

Magnolia the Bunny makes maps of the places
she's explored beyond the walnut grove.

And *Eleanor the Bear* gathers
flowers and plants to make tea for her friends.

Henry is a founding member
of the Walnut Animal Society,
an inventor, and a tinkerer.

You may have heard of his most famous invention, the Knot-A-Lot.

It's a device quite useful
for tying bow ties, which, as
you know, are very tricky to tie!

On this particular day, Henry was not inventing or tinkering.
He was looking.

Henry had lost an idea.

"Good morning, Henry!"

It was Eleanor the Bear. Henry was so busy looking for what he'd lost that he had forgotten all about their weekly cup of tea.

"What are you looking for?" asked Eleanor.

"My idea," said Henry. "I know it must be here somewhere."

"I am sure when you find it, it will be wonderful!" encouraged Eleanor. And then she suggested they go for a walk.

A walk seemed like as good an idea as any.
So Henry and Eleanor packed some snacks and
various necessities for finding things.

And then the two set out.

Henry and Eleanor went here.

And while they found lots of things,
they did not find what Henry was looking for.

And they went here.

But they still did not find what Henry was looking for.

As the sun began to set, Henry started to worry.
"Do you think I will ever find what I am looking for?"

"I know you will find it eventually," said Eleanor, ever hopeful.

Eleanor glanced at their knapsack and saw all the
things they did find that day. Then she looked at Henry.
He saw the treasures, too, and smiled at Eleanor.

Henry and Eleanor shared their last cookie and decided to head home.

All of a sudden, the darkening sky filled with the flickers
of tiny floating lights. Soon they were surrounded.

"Look!" shouted Henry.
A bright light landed atop Henry's head.
He could feel its warm glow.

"That's it!" he said. "I found what I was looking for!"

"A firefly?" asked Eleanor.

"My idea!" said Henry.

"Oh, Henry, it *is* wonderful," whispered Eleanor.

The two friends hurried home, little lights leading the way.

And back at the tree house,
Henry got right to work.